Mama Llama Says

Written and Illustrated
by Angela Larson

ISBN: 978-1-66783-827-4

Mama Llama says, "Eat your veggies."

Mama Llama says,
"Watch out for danger."

Mama Llama says,
"Hold still for your haircut."

Mama Llama says,
"Try to get along."

...but don't get into trouble."

Mama Llama says,
"Learn to   behave
like a proper llama."

Mama Llama says,
"Be helpful."

Mama Llama says, "Follow the Good Farmer."

Mama Llama says, "Good job!"

Mama Llama says,
"Time for bed."

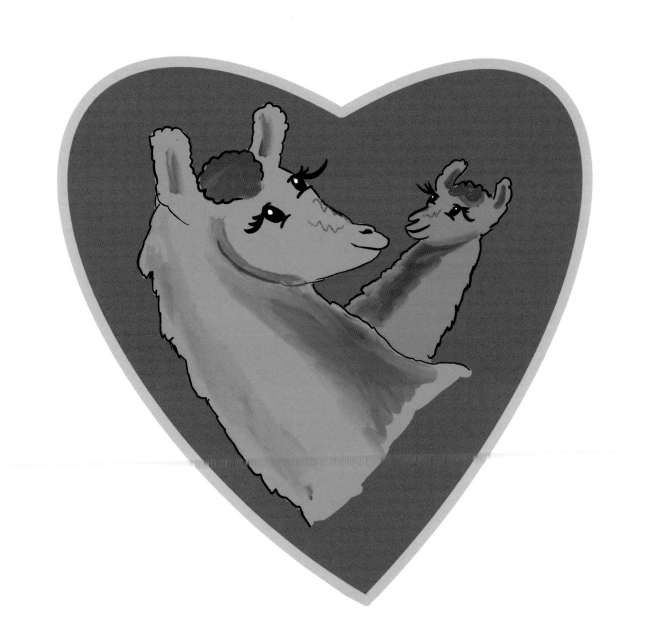

Mama Llama says,

"I love you!"

Did you know?

Llamas are part of the camelid family.
Their relatives include camels, alpacas, and guanacos.

A baby llama is called a cria.

Llamas are usually sheared once a year in early summer.

Llamas lay down with their legs tucked underneath them;
it's called "cushing."

Llamas living together all go to the bathroom in the same place.

Llamas spit when very upset or when they want others to go away.
The spit is made of partially digested grass and is very stinky!

Llamas make a humming noise when they are nervous or annoyed.